MIDDLE CHILD

Coleen Bickett

CONTENTS

1. | one

R ^{iah}

Free Ridge - Campbell Residence

Thursday - August 01

• • •

A lot can change in 3 months. And I do mean, a lot.

3 months ago I left Free Ridge with no intentions of coming back. I didn't tell anyone why and I left my brothers the saddest excuse of a "goodbye."

I just need some time to myself. I love you both so much.

No explanation, no details about where I was going or who I'd be with, nothing.

The last thing I needed was an audience to explain myself to my older brother. His friends littered my front lawn, most of them were from his gang. He's a Prophet. He was jumped in when he was just 17.

Some were smoking, some were lifting weights, others were just chilling. They all stopped what they were doing as soon as they realized it was me.

My older brother, Lando, stood upwhen he saw me. I couldn't tell if he was happy or pissed to see me, his face was unreadable.

All he had to do was nod his head and our front lawn was cleared within seconds leaving us alone.

"Hey," Was the first thing to come out of my mouth, I didn't know what else to say. The weight I was feeling on my chest lifted when Lando's serious face broke into a smile.

"Come here," He laughed as he pulled me into a tight hug. As much as it hurt, I didn't even care. I missed him and his beat hugs so much.

"I missed you, too."

He let go of me and looked down at me with tears in his eyes. The last time I saw him cry was when it found out our dad was murdered. Now that I think about it, that might have been the first time.

"You can't scare me like that." He sighed, he sounded relieved.

"I know, I'm sorry. I just, I felt like I was suffocating here."

Lando nodded his head, "I get it. Shit's been heavy lately. That all that's going on with you?"

It's like he had a radar when it came to me. Of course, he could tell something else was going on with me.

"Yeah," I lied even though I knew he knew I was lying.

"You've always been this way, you know? Miss Independent, always wanting to handle things on your own. You know you don't have to, right?"

I nodded my head, that's always been a problem for me. "I just hate putting my problems on other people, making my problems their problems."

"I don't see it that way. Keeping everything in ain't no good."

I snorted as I shook my head, "You're one to talk. When has Orlando Campbell ever talked about his feelings?" I asked, crossing my arms over my chest. The answer was never.

"Alright, you got me. We may be more alike that I realize. Just promise me you'll come to me next time instead of disappearing for 3 months. I don't care what it is, I got you, kid."

"Only if you promise you'll come to me." I said, holding my pinky out. Lando laughed before linking his pinky with mine. It was funny because his pinky was practically the side of my thumb.

"Now, I take pinky promises very seriously. Break a pinky promise, I break your pinky."

"And everyone thinks I'm the violent one," He laughed as he gave me a quick hug and kissed my forehead before walking off the porch.

"Where are you going? I just got back!" I called out, throwing my hands up.

"I got some business to handle. Don't worry, I'll be back before it's dark!" Lando called out to me before getting in his car and driving off.

I felt like I could finally breathe with that out of the way. Lando was the person I was most nervous about facing. Well, him and someone else. I checked my phone to see he still hadn't responded to my text about me being back in Free Ridge.

I dragged my suitcase into the house and went to my room to find it filled with clothes and shoes that didn't belong to me.

"What the hell?" I muttered out loud as I looked closer at one of the boxes of Jordan's sitting on my bed. They were a size 10, so I knew they belonged to LaTrelle.

I FaceTime'd him and he picked up on the first ring. "Riah! Wait, are you at home right now?"

"Yes! Now explain why all of your shit is in here!"

"Well, I didn't know if you were coming back and I needed a second closet," He shrugged.

—

After getting all of LaTrelle's things out of my room, we sat in the living room catching up with each other. I think I missed him the most. LaTrelle isn't just my little brother, he's my baby. I can't even describe the bond we have, it's just special. I'm the closest thing he has to a mother figure in his life.

"Who's been doing your hair while I was gone? These are nice," I said as I playfully pulled on one of his long braids.

"Just a girl from school," He tried to sound nonchalant, but he was fighting a smile.

"Just a girl? Seems like she's more than that." I sang teasingly.

"You remember Monse?"

"Mean ass Monse?" I asked. As long as I've known her, I think I've seen that girl smile twice.

"She ain't like that when you actually get to know her. She's pretty cool." His phone starting vibrating and her name scrolled across the screen.

With a heart emoji behind it.

"You mind if I take this?"

I shook my head, "Go ahead. Tell Monse I said heeeey." LaTrelle rolled his eyes before answering the phone and walking away.

"He has to walk away to talk on the phone," I thought out loud as I went to the kitchen for a snack. I checked my own phone to see my text still went unanswered. So, I decided to call instead.

It rang and rang until it finally went to voicemail. "Hey, Oscar. I know you haven't heard from me in a while, but...just call me, okay?"

Lando walked into the kitchen and I casually put my phone down. Judging from his demeanor, he didn't hear the voicemail I left or who I left it to.

"You still up?" He asked as he hopped up on the counter. "Yeah, me and LaTrelle were up talking. Did you know he was talking to Monse?"

"Of course I knew. I'm the one who tells him what to say to her! He ain't got no game," He chuckled.

"I've only been gone for 3 months, but it feels like so much longer." My laughter died down and my smile faded.

"You're back now, that's all that matters." His phone vibrated with a text and he read the message and sighed, "Fuck."

"What's wrong?"

"Nothing, I just gotta go. Prophet stuff." He hopped off the counter and kissed the side of my head before leaving.

Whenever he said "Prophet stuff," I knew not to ask questions. The less I knew, the better.

• • •

A/N: hey everyone! this is my first time publishing on wattpad in over a year! this story starts off kind of slow, but i promise, it'll pick up! votes and comments will be highly appreciated

if you made it this far, please vote

-charcoocheurie

2. | TWO

R iah

Free Ridge - Campbell Residence

Friday - August 02

...

I woke up the next morning and the first thing I did was check my phone. I had tons of miss calls and texts, but none from Oscar. I couldn't even blame him for ignoring him after what I did. I'd ignore me, too.

I yawned as I walked out of my room, stopping by LaTrelle's since his door was open.

"Lando home?" I asked, noticing how quiet the house was. He'd usually have music blasting from his room by this time.

"No, he didn't come home last night." He responded as he continued typing on his phone, probably sending a good morning text to Monse.

"Do you know where he went?"

He shrugged, "I think I heard him talking about meeting with a new connect. Something fell through with the Prophets old one."

"Wait," I said holding my hands up, "Why would Lando be meeting with the new connect? Only the leader can do that type of stuff." I didn't know much about how the Prophets operated, but I knew that much.

"And Lando's the leader now," LaTrelle said as if it was obvious, but that was news to me.

"Lando is leading the Prophets now?!"

LaTrelle looked up from his phone with his mouth hung open. "He didn't tell you?"

"No, he didn't."

—

LaTrelle felt bad about spilling the beans about my brother, so he took me out to lunch to try and make me feel better, but it didn't.

Every time I thought about my own brother leading the gang that got our father killed, I got sick to my stomach.

I took a bite out of my fry and threw it down, I wasn't hungry anymore.

"I'm sorry, Riah. I really thought you knew." LaTrelle apologized for the 100th time.

"You don't have to apologize, you didn't do anything wrong. Lando did."

"Come on, it's not like he had much of a choice. He's dad's oldest son, so he was next in line." I knew it was bound to happen eventually, but I just didn't want to believe it.

"Let's talk about something else, anything else." I sighed, not wanting to think about it any longer.

"Okay," LaTrelle started as he balled up his napkin, tossing it onto his empty plate, "I been wondering, where you been these past few months?" He pulled my plate towards him and helped himself to the rest of my food.

I knew they'd start asking questions eventually. "I was in the Bay Area," I responded honestly without giving too many details.

"Who you know out in the Bay Area?" He snorted. "A friend," I responded, taking the fry out of his hand and eating it.

"A friend?" He responded like Soulja Boy. "Is this friend a guy?"

"Why does it matter? I'm grown."I laughed at LaTrelle trying to check me.

"Yeah, you grown til' you see a spider," LaTrelle mumbled. I couldn't even say anything back because it was true. Spiders freak me the hell out, no matter how small they are.

I got a text and I immediately picked up my phone. It wasn't Oscar like I hoped, it was my best friend, Evelyn. I was a little letdown, but still happy to hear from her.

"You done? I'm gonna drop you off then I'm going to see Ev."

LaTrelle's face turned up into a hard frown the same way my face does when I hear my ex's name. "What's with the face?"

"We don't fuck with Evelyn no more." His face was serious, but I was having a hard time believing him.

"Wait, you're serious right now?" I laughed lightly.

"Dead serious, and you shouldn't either."

"Why not?" I wanted to know what Evelyn possibly could have done to make him feel that way.

"She's a Santo Hoe."

"A Santo Hoe?" I repeated back to him, trying to keep a straight face. "Yeah. Word on the street says she's been fucking around with Spooky."

I stopped laughing the minute he mentioned Spooky.

I knew him as Oscar, and before I left, we were together.

• • •if you made it this far, please vote

-charcoocheurie

3. | THᵣee

R iah

Free Ridge - Campbell Residence

Friday - August 02

• • •

"Riah!" Roz screamed as she ran up to me. All the bags on her shoulders were slowing her down and it was kind of hilarious. She was the type to pack like she was going on vacation when she was staying over for one night.

"Come here!" I laughed as I met her halfway. I wanted to catch up with her, so invited her to spend the night.

"I'm so glad you're back! Nobody puts up with my bullshit like you do," She sighed as we rocked back and forth. I couldn't wait to hear all about Roz and her shenanigans. I grabbed a bag from her and led her inside to my room.

She flopped down on my bed and turned to face me. "You have some explaining to do." I scrunched my face up after she tapped my nose.

"I know, I know, and I will explain myself," I said as I laid on my bed next to her, "But first, I need the tea on Ev. Is what everyone is saying about her true?" I whispered even though it was just us.

"Girllll," Roz sat up and crossed her legs, I knew I could count on her to tell me what's really going on. "I tried to tell her messing around with him was a bad idea, but she swore they weren't serious. It's just sex." She mocked Evelyn's voice perfectly.

"Next thing you know, he's all over to Instagram! This bitch brought back man crush Monday. How did you not see?"

Like we always say, once you post someone on your Instagram, it's serious.

I immediately pulled out my phone and re-downloaded Instagram. I deleted it and all my social media apps when I was gone because I was tired of people trying to reach out to me when I wouldn't respond to their texts.

After logging in, I ignored all the message alerts and requests to follow me and went straight to Evelyn's page. It might as well have been an Oscar fan page. All of her most recent pictures were either of him or them together.

_evelynelise

liked by callmeroz and 400 othersme: smile babe him: #mcm #mylil-babythatdontlisten_

"How long have they been together?" I asked out loud as I scrolled through the rest of her most recent pictures.

"Not that long. Maybe two months." Roz shrugged.

So they got together not even a month after I left. _

After a couple of movies and more than a couple of glasses of wine, Roz was knocked out on the couch holding a bag of chips like a teddy bear. I began cleaning up the mess we made when I finally got a text back.

Let's meet at our spot.

After an entire day, Oscar finally decided to hit me back.

I grabbed Roz's car keys off the table, careful not to make any noise. I snuck out of the house and drove her car to my old middle school. It's been abandoned since they closed it down a few years back.

I pulled up and parked next to Oscar's car. The door was propped open for me with a brick. I crept inside and made my way down the dark hallway. The only light came from the trophy case. I rounded the corner and walked down another hallway that led to the gym.

I followed the sound of the basketball bouncing until I found Oscar dribbling the ball. He stopped when I approached him. "Sorry it took so long to hit you back." He said without looking me in the eyes. He was acting weird and fidgety. He was nervous.

"Is it true?" I asked, getting straight to the point. I heard it from my brother and Evelyn and I saw it for myself on Instagram, but I needed to hear it from him.

"Is what true?" He asked, finally looking at me.

"I've known you long enough to know when you repeat someone's question back to them, you know exactly what they're talking about." He squeezed the ball between his hand and nodded his head.

"Yeah, me and Evelyn are together."

I felt like I got punched in the gut all over again. "What the hell is wrong with you?! She's my best friend, Oscar!" I shoved him, but he didn't budge. It was like pushing against a brick wall.

"I didn't think things would get serious between us!"

I scoffed and shook my head, "You two are serious? After a couple of months?"

"How was I supposed to know you were ever coming back?! You left and you didn't tell me shit. I texted you, I called you, I left you voicemails begging you to just let me know that you were okay."

Tears filled my eyes as I remembered those voicemails Oscar left me. Begging and pleading, on the verge of tears asking where I was and if I was okay, and I just listened to them and deleted them. I'd get fewer and fewer everyday until he just stopped leaving them.

"You ghosted me, Riah! What was I supposed to do? Just wait around until you decided you wanted to be with me? I asked you if you wanted to go all-in and be with each other for real, and you just.. ..disappear. I was ready to risk it all for you."

"I know you were, I was too..." I admitted. I contemplated telling my brothers and facing whatever consequences came from it, but I just couldn't bring myself to do it. Too much was on the line.

"Then why'd you leave?" Oscar asked, I could hear the heaviness in his voice and I could see the sadness plastered on his face.

"I..." I wanted to tell him the real reason why I left, to finally tell someone and get some of the weight off of my chest, but I couldn't. Not yet, at least. "It's complicated."

Oscar groaned and threw his hands up, "It always is with you."

My eyes watered again and I quickly blinked back the tears that were threatening to fall from my eyes. "I just wanted to apologize to you, face to face. I don't want there to be any bad blood between us. I don't want you to hate me," My voice cracked and I couldn't hold in my tears any longer. Oscar's face softened as he took a step forward.

"I could never hate you, Riah. Trust me, I tried," He laughed lightly.

We sat back onto the bleachers and sat in silence for a couple of minutes.

"You and Evelyn are a beautiful couple," I said breaking the silence. "She's a great person."

"I know," He agreed.

"Treat her well. She's had enough heartbreak in her life." I walked away before he could see the tears falling down my face.

I still loved him, and I had to watch him love someone else.

• • •if you made it this far, please vote

-charcoocheurie-charcoocheurie

4. | Four

O^{scar}

Free Ridge - Diaz Residence

Saturday - August 03

• • •

When I got back home I went straight to the kitchen, I needed a drink. I grabbed the bottle of tequila from on top of the fridge and took a swig from it, not bothering to get a glass. Seeing Riah had my emotions all over the place.

We were in love with each other. I never loved someone the way I loved her, not even Evelyn. After she left, I was devastated. I'd been in relationships before, but no one had ever broken my heart like she did.

Then I met Evelyn, and it didn't hurt as bad. She was sweet, funny, beautiful, all the things you'd want in a girl. In our short time together, I fell for her, but Riah was always in the back of my mind.

Even though Riah's back and I still have feelings for her, I have Evelyn now. I can't keep holding on to the hope that maybe she'll change her mind about us. It hurts too much.

"Babe, where'd you go? I woke up and you weren't there." I looked up and saw Evelyn standing there in one of my shirts rubbing her eyes.

"I just needed to handle something," I responded shortly.

"Something with the Santos?"

"Yeah," I knew she wouldn't ask any more questions if she thought I was out doing something for the Santos.

She walked over to me and ran her hand over my head, "You okay? You look like you got something on your mind."

Of course, I did, Riah. A half-naked, beautiful girl was right in front of me, and I still couldn't get Riah out of my head.

"Just you," I stood up and kissed her deeply, it caught her off guard. "Where did that come from?" She giggled as she pulled back.

"Does it matter?" I asked before kissing her again. This time, I pulled her closer to me and squeezed her ass. She didn't respond, she just continued kissing me. I guess it didn't matter to her.

I lifted her up and carried her back to my bedroom. I laid her on the bed and pulled down my sweats while she pulled down her thong. She moaned loudly when I pushed myself inside of her.

"Shh," I whispered in her ear, "Cesar's gonna hear us."

Evelyn nodded and put her hand over her mouth, muffling her moans. We stayed in that position for a few minutes before I felt myself getting closer.

"I'm gonna cum," I grunted seconds before it happened. I released myself deep inside of Evelyn before rolling off of her, lying flat on my back next to her on the bed.

She kissed my cheek before walking off to my bathroom. I sighed and covered my eyes with my hands.

I should not have been thinking about Riah while having sex with my girlfriend.

Riah

Free Ridge - Campbell Residence

Saturday - August 03

I couldn't sleep after I got back, I had too much on my mind. Instead of just sitting on the couch staring at the wall like I had been doing for the past few hours, I decided to get up and cook breakfast for everyone.

By the time I was done, I realized I went a bit overboard. There were eggs, bacon, pancakes, waffles, cinnamon rolls, sliced fruit, and even fresh-squeezed orange juice. It looked like I was feeding a football team instead of four people.

"Damn Riah," Roz said as she shuffled into the kitchen. She helped herself to a cinnamon roll. "You eating for two or something?"

"Very funny. You know my brothers can eat," I said as I began fixing plates for the both of them even though they probably wouldn't be up for another hour or so.

"Mm," Roz hummed as she got herself another cinnamon roll, "I'll call Ev. Now that girl can eat. I don't know where she puts it all away."

"I don't think that's a good idea," LaTrelle made it clear that he and Lando don't fuck with her anymore, and I'm pretty sure the rest of the Prophet's feel the same way. I'm starting to feel that way.

"Are you brothers seriously tripping that hard over Evelyn and Spooky that she can't even come over?"

"They doesn't trust her anymore. As far as they're concerned, her loyalty lies with Spooky and the Santos, now."

"So what does that mean for you and Evelyn? A lifelong friendship just down the drain over some guy?" Roz said waving her cinnamon roll around.

"I don't know," I huffed. There was more to it than that. Like getting over the fact that she was unknowingly dating my ex. She didn't do anything wrong, yet I couldn't get over the feeling of being mad at her.

"I'll just keep my distance for now."

"Free Ridge is small, babe. You can't avoid her forever."

I knew I couldn't, but I'd try anyway.

• • •How are we feeling about the book so for? Favorite character? Least favorite character? Predictions? Let me know in the comments!

Nine Votes For Next Update

-charcoocheurie

5. | Five

L ando

Free Ridge - Campbell Residence

Saturday - August 03

• • •

"Damn, it's like Christmas morning," I said as I walked into the kitchen. I knew Riah had to be the one who made all the food because I didn't and LaTrelle couldn't even boil water without burning it.

"You gotta try the waffles. I don't know how Riah does it, they're fluffy and crunchy at the same damn time, it's amazing," LaTrelle said before stuffing even more into his mouth. After grabbing my plate, I sat next to him at the table. "Where's Riah, anyway?" I asked as I drizzled syrup over my food.

"She left with Roz not too long ago. It's weird just seeing them two together without Evelyn."

It was weird not seeing all three of them together. Usually, when you saw one of them, the other two weren't far behind. It's too bad Evelyn ruined that for them. "Better get used to just seeing Riah and Roz together," I muttered as I cut my food. "Evelyn's dead to us."

We ate in silence for a while before LaTrelle spoke up, again. "Did Riah tell you where she went while she was gone?"

I shook my head, "Nah, I didn't ask. Why?"

"It's just...she told me she was with a friend in the Bay Area."

"Riah don't know nobody in the Bay Area," I frowned. "Exactly, but when Auntie Jackie visited us after dad died, she mentioned that mom moved to the Bay Area."

After our dad was killed, our mom left us when we needed her most. I still haven't forgiven her because what she did to us was unforgivable. "Riah wouldn't do that."

"I'm just saying, it makes more sense than some "friend" we never met," LaTrelle said before leaving the table.

I didn't press Riah about her leaving because I know how she is - the more you push, the more she shuts herself off, and that's the last thing I wanted.

I was cleaning up the kitchen when the front door opened. Riah came in with a few shopping bags in her hands. She took one look at me before rolling her eyes and heading to her room.

I sighed and tossed the towel in the sink before following her . I knew why she was mad at me, LaTrelle let it slip that I was leading the Prophets. It wasn't his fault though, it was mine for not telling her sooner.

"Riah, can we talk?" I asked as I stood in her doorway. "I have nothing to say to you." She said before slamming her door in my face. Yeah, she's pissed.

"Come on, I just got you back, I can't have you being mad at me already." I heard her sigh through the door before opening it.

"Was one funeral not enough? Now you're gonna leave me and La-Trelle to plan your funeral, too?"

"Don't be so dramatic. Nothing is gonna happen to me-"

"That's what dad would always say, see where that got him? Being a Prophet is one thing, but leading the gang?" She threw her hands up and shook her head before walking past me.

"I know it's risky, you don't think I know that?! Riah, I didn't have a choice." I tried to explain, but she wasn't trying to hear a word I had to say. She finally turned to face me and I saw that she was crying.

"Losing dad almost broke me. If I lost you, that would break me for sure." Seeing how upset she was had me on the verge of tears. I wrapped my arms around her and held her tightly.

"I'm not going anywhere, I swear. I'm not leaving you and LaTrelle alone. You're all I got."

• • •

How are we feeling about the book so for? Favorite character? Least favorite character? Predictions? Let me know in the comments!

if you made it this far, please vote

-charcoocheurie

6. | SIX

I held my phone to my ear as I waited for Riah to pick up her phone. Just like every other call, it went to voicemail.

I sighed and went to our messages and began typing.

Hey, just checking in, I know you're back. Let's meet up soon, I miss you. Love you

I sent the message and it joined all of the other messages I sent her that she didn't respond to. She's been back for about a week and she still hasn't hit me back.

At first, I assumed it was because she was overwhelmed, I knew I wasn't the only person wanting to see her after she was gone for 3 months.

Then, I started seeing her on Instagram hanging out with Roz almost everyday. It was hard not to feel some type of way about it. I love Roz, but before she even came along, it was always me and Riah.

I laid back in bed and pulled the covers up to my neck. I've been going though a lot lately and Riah's usually the one I go to. She knows things that no one else knows about me, not even Oscar.

"I thought you had to work today," Oscar said as he walked back into the room, well, his room. I've been staying here for a little over a month.

"My client canceled, she got into it with her man and he didn't want to pay for her to get her nails done anymore." He laughed and got into bed with me.

"That's messed up, but that means more time I get to spend with you."

"You don't have anything to do today?" A day off for Oscar was rare. "No, I'm all yours today. What you want to do?"

"I want to see my best friend, but she's ignoring me." I sighed. Oscar knew all about Riah and how she's been avoiding me lately.

"How about we go to the beach, clear our heads. I think it'll do us some good."

Going to the beach sounded a hell of a lot better than staying all bed in day waiting for a text back. _

It was hard to have a single worry at the beach. I laid back on my beach towel just listening to the waves and the music we had playing.

My relaxation was interrupted by phone ringing. I scrambled to pick it up thinking it was Riah, but it wasn't.

I declined the call and tossed my phone aside, annoyed. "Who was that?" Oscar asked, my phone landed right next to him.

"Spam call. I thought it was Riah," I sighed disappointingly.

"I thought we came here to get your mind off of her." He reminded me.

"I know, I know, I'm sorry."

He rolled onto his side and propped himself up to look at me, "Maybe it's best if you just let it go."

I lifted my sunglasses to I could really look at him, "You mean let go of my friendship of over 20 years? You're kidding, right?"

"I don't know, just seems like your putting a lot of energy into some-one who's not putting any energy into you."

I understood what he was saying, but he didn't understand me and Riah's relationship and just how much she meant to me.

Riah and her family were there through some of the darkest times in life. At one point, things got so bad that I lived with them. She was more like a sister to me, and Lando and LaTrelle were the brothers I never had.

Part of me thinks Riah is avoiding me because I'm with Oscar. It makes sense, she comes from a family of Prophets and Oscar leads the Santos. I never thought dating him would be as big of deal as everyone is making it.

I already accepted the fact that Lando and LaTrelle didn't want anything to do with me. What I couldn't accept was losing Riah, too.

RiahFree Ridge - Dwayne's JointFriday - August 16

"Hi, how can I help you?" Kierra, the owners daughter asked as I approached the counter.

"I'm picking up an order for Riah." LaTrelle convinced me to get Dwayne's joint for the 2nd day in a row. I wasn't complaining though, I couldn't get enough of the wings there.

Kierra handed me the bag and did a double take. "Riah, I thought that was you! I feel like I haven't seen you in months."

I tried handing her my card to pay for it, but she shook her head, "It's on the house."

"Thanks girl. What are you still doing on Free Ridge? Shouldn't you be at Spelman working on becoming the first female president?"

"First black female president," She corrected me, "And I don't want to leave my dad short staffed. My brother isn't exactly the most reliable," She nodded her head towards Jamal running through the front door.

"You're late."

"And your lace is lifting since we're staying the obvious!"

Kierra gasped and covered the frontal of her wig with her hand. Jamal wasn't lying.

"You wouldn't happen to be looking for a job?" She asked with a raised eyebrow.

"I am, actually." My last job wasn't exactly happy that I didn't show up for 3 months. Needless to say, they fired me.

"Come on, I'll put a good word for you with my dad!" She took my and pulled me to the back of the restaurant like a rag doll.

"Daddy," She sang as she poked her head in his office. "I have a surprise for you."

"Did you finally put out that garbage that's been sitting by the back door attracting flies for the last hour?"

"Even better, I got someone to replace me."

He looked up and smiled, "Riah, it's good to see you. How are you?"

"I'm good. You?"

"I'd be even better if my kids actually listened to what I said." He shot Kierra a look and she ignored it.

"She's great and I really think you should consider hiring her. I'll let you two talk business." She gave me shoulders a little shake before leaving us alone.

"Have a seat," I sat and laughed nervously, Kierra really put me on the spot.

"I'll be direct with you, Riah, I want to hire you, but," I got really excited just to get hit with the but.

"I worry about your brother's affiliation to the Prophets."

Of course he did. Even when my dad led the Prophets, people wanted to keep their distance from our family. It's fucked up because it has nothing to do with me, but I understand.

"Everyone knows Dwayne's Joint is neutral territory. The Prophets versus Santos bullshit has no place here, and I want it to stay that way."

"I understand, and I agree. I promise you, I don't want to come here and stir up any trouble. I just want to make a living like everyone else."

Mr. Turner nodded his head and sat silently for a moment.

"What's your shirt size?"

"Uh, medium."

He reached under his desk a tossed something to me. I unrolled it and saw it was a shirt.

"Welcome to the team, Riah. I'll show you around."

• • •

How are we feeling about the book so for? Favorite character? Least favorite character? Predictions? Let me know in the comments! if you made it this far, please vote

-charcoocheurie

7. | seven

R iah Free Ridge - Campbell ResidenceSaturday - August 24

I sat up in bed and immediately laid back down, I was sore from head to toe from working 5 days in a row at Dwayne's Joint. As badly as I wanted to turn around and go back to sleep, I forced myself out of bed.

I walked to the kitchen for a glass of water. Lando and LaTrelle were in there looking down at a box.

"What's that?" I yawned. Lando tossed the box to me and I caught to right before it hit the ground, "You got a package." He grumbled.

"Who pissed you off this morning?" I muttered as I turned to see who it was from. When I saw the name, it made sense why he sounded so upset.

It was from our mom.

"You lied to me," LaTrelle's scoffed. "You lied to both of us, straight to our faces."

"Because I knew you two would react like this! I get that leaving after dad died was a shitty thing to do, but she's still our mom!"

Lando shook his head, "What kind of woman leaves her kids when they need her most?"

"She was hurting too." When my mom first left, I felt the same way Lando felt. To be honest, I might have hated her even more than he did.

That all changed when I needed her. As bad our relationship was at the time, I knew I could always go to her. She told me things that my brothers had no idea about. If they knew, they'd understand.

"So that's an excuse to leave? You know what, I'm not even shocked that you're defending her, you did the same thing." His words cut me like a knife. You'd swear I was my brother's worst enemy by the way he was looking at me.

"Like mother, like daughter." Was the last thing he said before leaving me alone in the kitchen.

I wiped away the tears on my face and took a deep breath. I didn't even have time to process what just happened, I had to get ready for work.

Roz Free Ridge - Nelly's Nail SalonSaturday - August 24 • • •

"Hey beautiful," I sang as I approached Evelyn's station. She stared back at me with a blank face, not even cracking a smile.

"You're late. Now I have to push back my next appointment!" She complained.

"Cancel so you can come to the mall with me and you won't have that problem!"

"No," Evelyn took my hand and began filing off my old nail polish.

"Come on," I whined, "Who's the appointment for anyway?"

"Araceli."

I smacked my lips and rolled my eyes, Araceli is the worst client ever. Ev complains about her all the time. "You know you don't want to her nails,"

She ignored me and continued filing my nails, "What design you want this time?"

"Araceli's gonna complain the whole time, and when you're done, she's gonna say she doesn't like them. Then, you're gonna feel bad and you're gonna charge her half the price Then she's gonna post them on Instagram talking about how much she's loves them later. Aren't you tired of getting scammed by that bitch?"

Evelyn stopped what she was doing and scoffed, "She does do that every time."

"And she doesn't tip," I reminded her.

"Fuck that," Evelyn muttered as she began typing out a message on her phone, "Hey, babe. So sorry, but I have to cancel, something unexpected came up..." She read out loud as she typed.

"Looks like my afternoon just cleared up."

—

"This top with this purse, or, this top with this purse?" I asked holding up the two purses to my chest. Evelyn tapped her chin as she thought about it, "Both." We said at the same time. This is why I love Evelyn, she encourages my shopping addiction.

I put both purses on my arm as we continued looking around the store. "Can I ask you something?"

"Yes, I think are Oscar are going to be together forever and ever." I snorted as I picked out a dress and held it against my body.

"I'm being serious, Roz." I could tell by her voice something was bothering her, so I got serious, too.

"Okay, I'm sorry. What's up?"

"Is Riah ignoring me on purpose or am I tripping?"

"She's been...busy," I lied, hoping she would buy it, but she didn't. "She's working at Dwayne's Joint now, I barely have time to see her."

"Bullshit! I see you two together almost everyday on her IG story!" I couldn't argue with that.

"She's just....keeping her distance for now." I admitted.

"Keeping her distance? Why? Because I'm dating Oscar?" She scoffed.

"In her defense, her brother is leading the Prophets. Running around town with the enemy's girl isn't exactly a good look."

"The enemy's girl? That's who I am now?!" She laughed, not because what I said was funny, but because she was getting upset. "So I'm not even Evelyn, your best friend since kindergarten. I'm the enemy's girl, now."

"That's not what I meant. I'm just saying," I sighed and threw my hands up, "Fuck, I don't know what I'm saying. Don't listen to me," I said, trying to remove myself from the deep shit I was in. I learned a long time ago getting between Riah and Evelyn when they were fighting always ended bad.

"Okay. I won't listen to you, I'll listen to Riah instead. She can ignore my texts all she wants, but she can't ignore me in person."

"Evelyn!" I called out to her as she started walking away, but she just ignored me.

I looked back and forth between her and the two purses on my arms, "Dammit, Ev," I muttered as I dropped the purses on a table before running after her.

• • •just a reminder that more votes = faster updates. so, if you read, please vote if you made it this far, please vote

-charcoocheurie

8. | EIGHT

R iah Free Ridge - Dwayne's Joint Saturday- August 24• • •

"Barbecue brisket sandwich with onion rings and a bacon cheese burger with fries." I placed the plates down in front of the customers and they both just stared at me like I had a second head.

Kierra came behind me and took the plates and brought them to the customers and the table behind me. I sighed and walked back to the kitchen, I'd been making stupid mistakes like that all day. Between feeling like shit and that argument with my brothers that morning, I couldn't focus on a thing.

"Hey, you good?" Kierra snuck up on me and I jumped. "Yeah, yeah, I'm fine." I nodded my head a little too hard, making my head hurt.

"You sure? You've been off all day."

I nodded my head, "I'm just a little tired, that's all."

"Take few minutes to yourself while we're not busy," She suggested, but I shook my head. "No, I'm fine, I swear-"

"Take a break." Kierra was on the debate team back in high school l so I knew better than to go back and forth with her.

"Fine," I grumbled. I sat at an empty booth and wrapped utensils to busy myself. I had only wrapped a few before I swore I heard someone calling my name. The voice sounded just like Evelyn's.

"Riah!"

I knew I wasn't crazy. I turned around and saw Evelyn walking towards me and Roz following behind her trying to keep up.

"What's going on?" I asked, looking between the two of them.

"We need to talk," Evelyn responded.

"About...?"

"The way you've been ignoring me since you got back. You've been with Roz almost everyday since you got back and you never even texted or called me once."

"I was going to," I began to explain, "I just needed some time."

"Time for what? To find a way to tell me we can't be friends anymore because I'm dating a Santo and your brother's a Prophet?!"

I looked at Roz and she mouthed sorry.

"Evelyn, we're not doing this right now."

"Why not?!"

"Because you're doing the most and you're causing a scene at my job! You need to leave." This was the shit Dwayne was talking about. I needed her gone before he came out of his office and heard what was going on.

Evelyn scoffed and shook his head. "Fine, I'll leave."

"Thank you." I huffed.

"If you can look me in my eye and tell me that's not the reason why you've been ignoring me."

Evelyn and her bullshit was making my head throb. I took a deep breath and grabbed into the table because I felt like I was about to fall over.

"You can't even do that," Evelyn scoffed. "We've been friends since kindergarten and this is how you treat me? There has never been a time that you needed me and I wasn't there, no matter what. You are the last person I thought would react this way..."

Evelyn's voice seemed to get further and further away even though she was standing right in front of me. I felt hot and cold at the same time. Something was wrong.

"Riah? Riah?" The sound of Roz's voice echoed. I was standing and the next thing I knew, I was staring at the ceiling and everyone was standing around me.

if you made it this far, please vote

-charcoocheurie

9. | Nine

LaTrelleFree Ridge - Finnie ResidenceSaturday - August 24 • • •

"I just can't believe she lied to us like that. To make things worse, she was with our mom the whole time she was gone." I vented to Monse as we walked through the neighborhood. After that fight with Riah this morning, I needed someone to talk to.

"Maybe I missed something, but why was Riah staying with your mom a problem?"

"Because my mom abandoned us when we needed her most. She dipped after our dad got killed." I swallowed hard, fighting the urge to cry. "It should have been her, not him."

"Hey," Monse stopped walking and grabbed my arms, "I used to feel the same way about my mom, but now that she's gone, I wish I would have given her the chance to explain herself. Everybody makes mistakes, even parents."

"Shit, I forgot, I'm sorry." I was so busy ranting about my mom that I forgot Monse lost her mom about a year ago. "You don't need to apologize you just need to have a little empathy."

"I wouldn't even know where to start. I've been so mad at her for so long that's all I know how to do." I sighed as I looked down at her. "What would you do if you were me?"

"If I were in your size 10 shoes," Monse laughed, I loved her laughed, "I would write her a letter telling her exactly how you feel, don't hold anything back. But don't send it to her. Just start by getting all those feelings out." She explained. Writing down how I felt did sound a hell a lot easier than talking about it. I was never great about talking about my feelings.

"Has anyone ever told you that you give really good advice?"

She flipped her hair over her shoulder and smirked, "You weren't the first and you definitely won't be the last." We stopped walking when we got to her house. "Call me later?"

"Yeah, I will." I responded lingered in my place, looking into her deep brown eyes. The way the sun was hitting her was literally making her glow. I couldn't stop myself from staring. She held her hand over her mouth as she started giggling, it was the cutest shit ever.

"Why are you still in front of my house?"

"Because I really don't want to leave without a kiss."

Monse took a step forward closing the gap between us. She got on her toes and wrapped her arms around my neck, "Then don't."

Her lips collided with mine and we kissed as if we'd done it hundreds of times before. Our first kiss together was interrupted by my phone vibrating in my pocket for the 5th time in an hour. I was ignoring the calls because I was with Monse.

"Seems like someone is trying really hard to get in touch with you," She muttered, her lips brushing against mine. I pulled my phone out my pocket just enough to see that it was Lando blowing me up. "It's just my brother."

I tried to resume our kiss, but Monse playfully pushed my face away, "Let's stop before we get carried away."

"What if I wanna get carried away?" She tried to play like I was getting on her nerves, but she liked that shit.

"Goodbye, LaTrelle." She sang as she closed the gate and walked to her house. I waited until she got inside to leave. As I was walking home, I called Lando back to see what was so important.

"Where the hell are you?!" Lando barked into the phone as soon as the call connected. I frowned and pulled the phone from my ear and put it on speaker instead. "I'm heading home, I was walking Monse home. Why?"

"Riah's in the hospital!"

I froze when I heard him say that, already assuming the worst. "What happened?" I asked, trying my best to stay calm. All I could think about was how I treated her that morning.

"I don't know. Roz texting me and told me she's in the hospital, but she didn't say anything else. I'm about to head over there to see for myself."

"I'm on the corner of Freemont and Clearview, pick me up on your way there."

Seconds later, I heard an engine roaring behind me. Lando pulled his car over and I hopped in before he sped off towards the hospital. I wasn't the most spiritual person, but I prayed that my sister would be alright. I needed the chance to apologize and make things right.

LandoFree Ridge - Free Ridge Community HospitalSaturday - August 24• • •

I ran into the hospital frantically looking for a familiar face, LaTrelle wasn't far behind me. I found Roz sitting in the waiting area pacing back and forth.

"Roz!" Her head snapped up and she jogged towards me. "What happened? You never texted me back."

"Sorry, my phone died. I texted you from Evelyn's phone and you never texted back." It made sense that I never got the message because I blocked her number when I found out about her and Spooky. I blocked her on everything.

"It never came through. Where's my sister? What happened to her?"

"We were at Dwayne's Joint and she fainted out of nowhere. Nobody's updated us yet." She sighed, pulling her hair back into a ponytail and letting it go.

I blew air into my cheeks and took a seat in one of the peeling chairs. I was trying to stay positive, but it was hard, especially when so many bad things had been happening to me and my family.

"Here, I got you a charger." I looked up when I heard a familiar voice. I immediately recognized it was Evelyn's. To make matters worse, Spooky was with her.

"What the fuck are they doing here?" I asked no one in particular. Evelyn avoided eye contact with me while Spooky mugged me.

"Lando, now is not the time," Roz whispered as she pushed me towards a corner. "Evelyn was there when it happened, she's just as worried about Riah as you are. She's not here's to start trouble."

"Then why roll up with him?" I shamelessly pointed to Spooky, not giving a damn if he saw. It wasn't like his bitch ass was going to do anything, anyway.

"Probably because she doesn't feel safe anymore! You got all the Prophets calling her a traitor and a Santo Hoe. I wouldn't roll up here alone either if I was her." Roz whispered. "For the sake of your sister, please chill."

I didn't want to, but I agreed. "Thank you." Roz sighed. I followed her back to the waiting area and took a seat directly across from Spooky. We stared each other down, but neither of us said a thing. Something about him being there just didn't sit right with me.

He shouldn't be here.

• • •

if you made it this far, please vote

-Charcoocheurie

10. | Ten

Riah Free Ridge - Community Hospital Saturday - August 24 ...

I woke up in a cold hospital room and an IV in my arm. I tried sitting up, but I immediately laid back down because it was too painful. It felt like someone dragged a knife across my lower abdomen.

The nurse writing on her clipboard stopped when she noticed I was awake, "I'll get Dr. Turner."

A couple of minutes later, Dr. Turner, who just happened to be my boss Dwayne's wife, walked into the room and closed the door.

"Riah, how are you feeling?" She asked as approached the bed.

"I've felt better. I guess I was a little dehydrated," I laughed lightly pointing to the IV.

"You're more than a little dehydrated. The stitches from your C-Section bursted, causing an infection. That's why you fainted today."

I had been feeling pain around my scar, but I assumed it was because I was on my feet all day working.

"You're only 8 weeks postpartum, you should be taking it easy, not working 12 hour shifts at my husband's restaurant." I felt like a kid getting scolded by my mother.

"I know," I exhaled deeply, "I just thought if I came back and did everything I would normally do, nobody would suspect a thing."

"No one knows you had a baby?" I shook my head, the only person who knew was my mom, and the doctor who delivered my baby, of course.

When I found out I was pregnant, I was already almost half way through the pregnancy. When I was starting to show, I didn't have enough time to figure things out, so I left to give myself some time. I didn't even tell Oscar.

"I'm going to prescribe you some antibiotics that will clear that infection right up. Now you have to promise me that you'll take it easy for a couple of weeks. If I even see you within 10 feet of Dwayne's Joint, I'll escort you home myself." Dr. Turner warned sound like like a true mom.

"I promise, I won't." Two weeks off didn't sounds like the worse thing in the world. I honestly needed the break.

Dr. Turner patted my leg and gave me a warm smile, " Take care, Riah."

She was about to walk out of the room, but I stopped her, "Wait, Dr. Turner," She turned around and returned to the bed.

"I can't have it getting out that I had a baby, I'm not ready for everyone to know that yet."

"Oh, honey, I couldn't tell anyone even if I wanted to. Doctor Patient confidentiality."

"So you can't repeat anything I say?" I asked raising an eyebrow. She shook her head, "Not unless I want to lose my license, and I don't plan on doing that because I have two kids to put through college."

Since she couldn't say anything, it seemed like to perfect time to get a few things off my chest...

"So a couple of years ago I started dating Oscar even though he's a Santo and my dad was leading the Prophets at the time. I really wanted to come clean about our relationship and stop sneaking around, but I was just waiting for the right time. Then, my dad got killed, so it really wasn't a good time to do it. Then I found out I was pregnant. So I left Free Ridge and stayed with my mom in Oakland until I had the baby. I came back a few weeks ago with the intention to tell Oscar about the baby, but I came back to find out he's dating my best friend. She didn't know about me and Oscar, but I still can't get over being mad at her, and Oscar didn't think I'd ever come back so I shouldn't really be mad at him either. I just don't know what to do."

I leaned back on the pillows after getting all of that out in what felt like a single breath. Dr. Turner's mouth was hung open.

"Sorry, I didn't mean to unload all of that on you. I just needed to tell someone."

"No, no, you don't have to apologize. That's a lot for one person to carry. Are you okay?"

Her asking me if I was okay triggered me because as much as I pretended I was, I was far from it. I couldn't even tell her I wasn't, all I could do was cry.

Dr. Turner held me as my cry turned into full on sobs. "It's okay, let it all out." She whispered as she rocked me gently.

Oscar

It was almost midnight and we were still at the hospital. I was in the hallway while Evelyn was in the room with Riah. I was freaking out inside, but I couldn't show it. I just wanted to see that Riah was okay for myself.

Evelyn finally came out of the room and I was able to catch a glimpse of Riah before the door shut. She was curled up in the bed like she was about to fall asleep. "She staying here by herself tonight?" I asked, worrying that she was going to be alone. She had a thing about hospitals, she hated them.

"No, her brothers are taking Roz home then they'll be right back." She smiled. "So I'm guessing you and Riah are good?" She nodded, "Yeah, I think we're going to be alright. We had a long talk about what's been going on and we both agreed that our friendship is more important than some stupid gang beef."

I put my arm around her and kissed the side of her head, "I'm glad you got your girl back." I really was glad they worked it out, Evelyn was going crazy behind the whole situation.

"Me too," Evelyn responded as she wrapped her arms around me. We got to my car and I opened the door for her. When I got into the drivers side, I started patting myself down looking for my phone.

"I think I left my phone in the restroom. I put it down to wash my hands. I'll be right back."

"You sure? I can call it-" I shut the door and jogged towards the entrance before Evelyn could hear my phone vibrating in my pocket. I lied about leaving it behind so I could see Riah.

I scanned the hall to make sure her brothers weren't around. I quietly cracked the door and went in when I knew for sure she was alone. She was curled up in a ball on her side sleeping.

I didn't want to wake her, so I bent over and kissed her forehead. "I love you." I whispered.

• • •

if you made it this far, please vote

-Charcoocheurie

11. | ELEVEN

RiahFree Ridge - Campbell Residence Sunday - August 25•••

Dr. Turner discharged me this morning, and I've never been happier to be home. I went to the kitchen to reach for a glass and LaTrelle came running behind me. "I got it, sis."

I sighed leaned on the counter while he got a glass of water for me. He's taking Dr. Turner's advice to take it easy more seriously than I am.

"Thank you for the water," I tipped my glass to him before going to my room.

I closed my door and picked up the package from my mom that I never got to open.

I opened the box and there was a handwritten letter on top.

Hopefully it still smells like him by the time it gets to you. I'm sure you miss him as much as he misses you.

-Ma

Underneath the letter was a small blanket. I held it to my nose and inhaled deeply, my eyes immediately filled with tears. It smelled just like my son.

I clutched the blanket to my chest and the tears just rolled down my face. I need to see him.

Someone knocked on my door and I quickly hid the note and the blanket under my bed before I dove into it, pulling my covers over me. "Come in!"

The door creaked open and it was Lando.

"I just wanted to check on you. You need anything? I can cook something for you."

"I'll pass, your cooking might send me back to the hospital," I joked, finally making him smile. "It's not that bad," He laughed before walking over and sitting at the edge of my bed.

"I'm really sorry for what I said to you yesterday. I just didn't under-stand why you would forgive her. I still don't." He sighed.

"Did you ever ask mom why she left?"

"She left because she's selfish and-"

"No, Lando, that's the reason you came up with," I said cutting him off, "Did you ever ask her yourself?"

He simply shook his head, "No."

"Well I did. She felt responsible for dad getting murdered."

Lando looked at me and frowned, "She felt responsible? She's not the one who pulled the trigger, why would she feel that way?"

I inhaled and exhaled deeply because it wasn't easy to talk about. "That night, the night that dad was murdered, he and mom got into a fight. It was bad, mom said it was the worst fight they ever had. She told him to leave, so dad left, and he never came back. Mom left because she couldn't look us in the face knowing she was the reason we didn't have a dad anymore. That's why she left."

Lando sniffed and quickly wiped his eyes, "How was she supposed to know that was going to happen to him? It wasn't her fault."

"That's what I've been trying to tell her, but she's not convinced."

"I'm glad she still has you. She needs somebody now that dad's gone." I nodded my head, we needed each other more than ever.

"I was actually gonna head back to spend the week with her. You can come, too. She misses you, a lot."

She always says how much Angelo reminded her of how Lando was when he was a baby. He's a carbon copy of Oscar, but he has my brother's eyes.

Lando looked like he might actually say yes for a moment, but he shook his head, "I don't think I'm ready for all that. I can give you a ride, though."

"I'd like that."

—

"Ma, where are you?" I shouted when I walked into my mom's house and didn't see her in her usual spot on the couch. She came running around the corner shushing me.

"I just got him down," She whispered. "My bad," I whispered back to her. I went over to the spare room that she turned into Angelo's nursery. I had to fight the urge to take him out of his crib and cuddle him. The only reason I didn't was because I knew it could be hell to get him back to sleep.

Instead of waking him up, I gently kissed his head. I met my mom in the kitchen so we could talk without disturbing him.

"I tell you what Riah," My mom glanced over her shoulder as she stirred her pot, "You made one beautiful baby."

"I sure did." I smiled to myself. Angelo didn't even go through that weird wrinkly old man phase that most babies go through, he's been a cutie.

"He's bright, too."

"I know right, he's so smart already." Every mom thinks their kid is the cutest and the smartest, but mine actually is.

"My grand baby is smart, but that's not what I meant. That's one bright skin baby."

"What does his completion have to do with anything?"

"All I'm saying is you're a caramel complexion and Dez is dark choco-late, How'd you end up with a vanilla ass baby?" She asked with her arms crossed over her chest.

"Ma!"

"What?! You state the obvious these days and everyone wants to cancel you." She scoffed rolling her eyes.

"Dez isn't his father." I hadn't exactly told my mom who Angelo's father is yet. The space for the father on his birth certificate is blank.

"I figured that out when I saw that good hair on his head," My mom said before turning back to stir her pot again.

"There's no such thing as good hair, Ma. All hair is good hair."

"You know what I mean! He's got that El DeBarge hair like he's mixed with something. Wait a minute, please tell he that baby's daddy ain't white!" She said it so dramatically as if Angelo's dad being white would be the end of the world.

"His dad isn't white, he's Mexican."

"Is there a reason you're being so secretive about who his father is?"

I sighed and nodded my head. "He's a Santo. If Lando and the other Prophets find out, who knows what kind of hell will break lose."

My mom looked both surprised and disappointed at the same time. "A Santo, Riah? Really?"

Angelo started crying and I got up to go and get him, "You should know better than anybody that you can't help who you fall in love with."

Even though my dad and Oscar were in different gangs, the point was, they were still in gangs. My mom fell in love with my dad and I fell in love with Oscar.

• • •New Character: Angelo

• • •

if you made it this far, please vote

-Charcoocheurie

12. | Twelve

Oscar walked into the kitchen and reached for one of the cookies cooling on the pan, but I slapped his hand away. "These are for Riah's basket. Those are yours," I pointed to the cookies I put aside for him because I know he has a sweet tooth.

"Basket? What basket?" He asked as he ate his cookie.

"The basket with all of Riah's favorite things. Chocolate chip cookies, fuzzy socks, candles, fruit punch jarritos, cool ranch Doritos, and her favorite season of Bad Girls Club on dvd. I'm gonna bring it by her house after I get some balloons at the store." I explained excitedly. After our talk at the hospital, I think things are finally gonna go back to normal between me and Riah.

"Look, I know you and Riah made up, but that doesn't mean everything is magically fine. I don't think it's a good idea for you to go to her house alone."

"I'm just going to her house and back," I groaned as I put her cookies into a small bag. "Yeah, her house that's in the middle of Prophet territory! It's not safe!" Oscar shouted as he followed me around the kitchen.

"Oscar, please! Just stop. You're making this a bigger deal than it is." I grumbled as I carried the basket past him towards the door. "Evelyn!" He call out to me, but I just grabbed my keys and went to my car.

He called me on my phone a few times, but I just ignored it. I didn't feel like hearing him try and talk me out of going to Riah's house.

I parked on the curb and grabbed the basket out the passenger seat before going to the door. I knocked a few times and Lando answered the door.

"What you doing here, Evelyn?"

"I made a basket for Riah with all her favorite things." I smiled and did a little dance with the basket, but he just stared at me. "Is she here?" I tried to look past him into the house, but he stepped out and closed the door.

"No, and even if she was, I wouldn't let her see your trifling ass."

I wish LaTrelle would have answered the door instead...

"Lando, I get why you're mad at me, but don't you think you're going a bit much?"

He laughed and ran his hand over his mouth, "I'm doing a bit much? Kind of like you were doing a bit much when you were messing around with me and Oscar at the same time?"

I knew he was still hurt over how the situation between us ended, but I never imagined he'd take this this far. He's the reason my life has been a living hell. All the Prophet's are following his lead. If he would tell them to leave me alone, they would, but he's enjoying how hard he's making my life.

We weren't even dating.

"Lando, please-"

"I told my boys about you and you fucking embarrassed me."

"I'm sorry, I-"

"You need to leave, Evelyn."

I sat the basket down on the doorstep and turned to walk away. The Prophets on the porch next door followed me and barked like dogs until I got to my car and drove away with tears in my eyes.

Riah Oakland Friday - August 30

I held Angelo as he slept in my arms, he fell asleep while I was feeding him his bottle. My brother would be here to bring me back to Free Ridge soon.

"Leaving you gets harder and harder every time," I whispered, holding back my tears. "But one day, I won't have to leave you anymore. I'll get to see that beautiful face every single day." I tapped his nose with my finger and he smiled in his sleep.

My plan is to save enough money to get a place of my own where me and Angelo can live comfortably, far away from all the bullshit in Free Ridge. I want Oscar to come with us too, but I don't think that's gonna happen now that he's dating Evelyn. We can't be the happy family I thought we'd be.

"Baby," My mom knocked on the door lightly, "Lando's parked outside." I carefully handed Angelo off to her before gathering my things.

"I'll be back soon," I kissed my mom's cheek before leaving. Leaving Angelo felt like I was leaving a peace of me behind.

"You okay?" My brother asked me. "No," I answered honestly as tears fell down my cheeks faster than I could wipe them. "You wanna talk about it?"

I shook my head, "No, just drive."

-I slept for most of the ride home. When Lando pulled into the driveway, balloons coming out of the trashcan caught my attention.

Instead of going straight inside, I went to the trashcan to see what the balloons were about. I was surprised to see a basket wrapped in plastic filled with stuff. Not just random stuff, but things I loved. I pulled off the envelope and read what was written inside.

Riah,

I hope this basket of all your favorite things makes your down time not suck so bad. I'm glad we cleared the air between us, I love you more than you know.

P.S. if you need someone to watch season 13 of bad girls club with, I'm just a call away.

-Ev

I pulled the basket out of the trashcan and carried it inside. Evelyn's actually been trying and I've been shutting her down time after time. I've been such a terrible friend to her lately, and it's time to change that.

I picked up my phone and called her, she picked up on the first ring. "Hey, is everything okay? Are you okay?"

"Yeah, I'm fine. I just wanted to know if you wanted to watch bad girls club with me?"

There was a long pause on the line and for a second I thought she hung up. "Ev? You there?"

"Yeah, yeah, I'm here. I'd actually love that." It was like I could hear her smiling through the phone.

"You can come over now, actually. My room is a bit of a mess, but-" I was in the middle of inviting her over when she cut me off.

"How about you come over instead?"

"Okay. Give me about 20 minutes and I'll be right over."

"Perfect. Just one more thing, I'm not home. I'll send you my location."

Before I could ask where she was, she ended the call. A few seconds later she texted me her location. I didn't immediately recognize the address, if I had, I probably wouldn't have gone.

• • •

if you made it this far, please voteAlso, thank for reading

-Charcoocheurie

13. | THIRTEEN

Free Ridge - Diaz ResidenceSunday - August 25 • • •

I don't know why it didn't click that the address Evelyn set me was Oscar's. It should have, I'd been to his house countless times.

Evelyn came running out of his house to meet me at my car. "Riah!" She hugged me tightly and I groaned, I was still sore from Dr. Turner restitching my c-section scar.

"Sorry, I just got excited." She laughed nervously. "Come on, I made those mini cream puffs you like!" She grabbed my hand and dragged me across the street to the house.

"You can sit on the couch, I'll be right back." She went to the kitchen leaving me alone. The living room was pretty much exactly the way it was last time I was here, down the to the missing cushion on the couch and the ash tray on the table that always seemed to be full.

"Do you wanna start from episode 1 or do you wanna skip to the episode when everyone wants to beat Natalie's ass?" She asked as she walked into the living room with the tray of cream puffs.

"Why are we here and not at your house?" I asked. I didn't mean to ignore her question, but it felt weird being at Oscar's house when we weren't together, especially since he wasn't there.

Evelyn shifted uncomfortably on the couch and exhaled loudly. "My mom lost another job and I don't make enough doing nails to make the payments on my own and....long story short, we lost the house. My mom went to stay with my aunt until she figures something out. I didn't go because I'd be too far from the shop, so Oscar let me stay with him."

Evelyn's mom has been unstable her entire life. Ever since she was a kid, it was like she was the parent and her mom was the kid.

"I'm really sorry that happened. Is there anything I can do to help?" Evelyn shook her head and quickly wiped her eyes. "No, I don't need anything from you. I just need a friend." She sniffed.

I smirked and grabbed a cream puff before grabbing the remote, "Let's skip to the episode where everyone wants to beat Natalie's ass."

"Now that I think about it, that's every episode." Evelyn pointed out making us both laugh. I missed laughing with her. I missed her.

• • •

We were in the middle of another episode of Bad Girls Club when the front door opened. Oscar froze when he saw me. I had to be the last person he expected to see when he got home.

"Hey babe," Evelyn tilted her head back and Oscar leaned down to kiss her. I felt weird watching them kiss, I felt like I was watching my parents share a kiss. Bleh.

"You two haven't officially met, have you?" She asked looking between the two of us. We both just shook our heads. "Oscar, this is Riah, Riah this is Oscar."

Pretending to be strangers was harder than I thought it would be.

"Nice to meet you," I smiled softly. "Same here. I won't bother you two. If you need me, I'll be out back." He silently left, I waited until I heard the backdoor slide and close before I spoke.

"Why didn't you tell me this was Spooky's house?"

"Because I knew you wouldn't come if I did. I'm sorry I didn't tell you, I just really wanted to see you."

"I wanted to see you too. You could have come over to my place, you know?"

Evelyn shook her head, "No, I couldn't. Earlier Lando made that very clear." She mumbled as she gathered our plates and brought them to the kitchen, I followed behind her.

"Wait, you were at my house earlier?"

"Yeah," Evelyn glanced up at me, "I went over to bring you that basket and Lando answered the door. I asked him if you were home and he said even if you were, he wouldn't let you see my trifling ass."

Yeah, definitely something Lando would day.

"I'm surprised he didn't throw that basket in the garbage," She snorted. I would tell her that he did, but I decided not to. He's already put her through enough.

"Yeah, me too." I muttered.

Oscar walked into the kitchen to get a beer. I couldn't tell he was forcing himself not to look in my direction. "Doesn't matter, though. You're always welcomed here. Right babe?"

Evelyn wrapped her arms around his waist and he finally looked at me as he took a swig from his beer. "Anytime."

Oscar Diaz Residence • • •

Roz got a phone call and stepped outside, leaving me and Riah alone. "You scared me the other night." I sighed as I went for another beer. I was so anxious around her I needed something to calm me down.

"I scared myself," She muttered, "I'm good, though. I just gotta slow down, that's all."

A silence fell between us before I thought of something else to say. I could have walked away, but I wanted to talk to her. "I'm glad you and Ev are back on good terms."

"So I am. I didn't realize how much I missed her..." She trailed off, looking around until her gaze finally met mine.

Beautiful as ever.

"Why are you looking at me like that?" I didn't realize how hard I was staring until she pointed it out. "What? I can't look?" She put her head down as she laughed.

"You can't look at me like that anymore," Her smile faded and she actually sounded pretty said. I guess you can say I was still having a hard time accepting that we were really over.